8 7
M A R S
HUGHES ELECTRIC
411 S. CLINTON ST. SYRACUSE NY
3460 1230
3460 2190
LOVE
New York Public Library
BIRTHDAY
SPARE TIME to Strike up party!
for Penny's Bowling Bash
Saturday December 27th
3:00 - 5:00 pm
union square lanes
NYC
FATTA CUCKOO

MAIN DRAG MUSIC BROOKLYN
BACK TO SCHOOL?
$5 OFF ANY HAIRCUT
ANY STYLE

DINER

FRANCE

LOVE YOUR OCEANS

ECONOMY CANDY

MIXED GREENS
NY

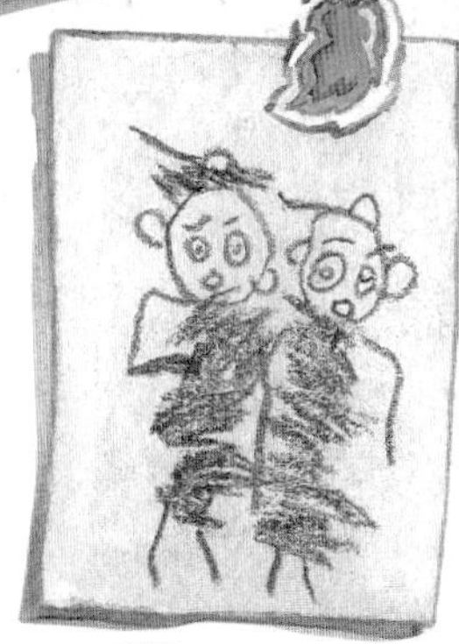

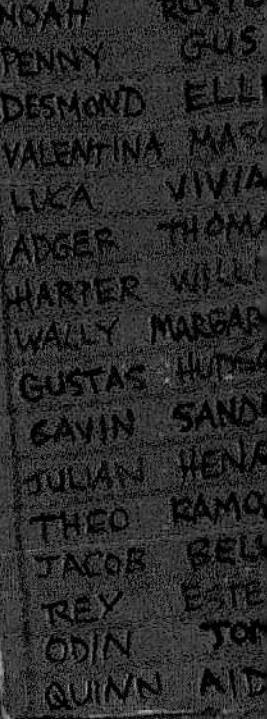
MARS
SEBASTIAN
SCHEI
SUNNY
TOMMY
NOAH
PENNY
DESMOND
VALENTINA
LUCA
ADGER
HARPER
WALLY
GUSTAS
GAVIN
JULIAN
THEO
JACOB
REY
ODIN
QUINN

RISD

OBEY

R
LOUIS
RESTAURANT
286 Brook St Providence RI

X O X O

To Charlotte, Ben,
Will, and Eve.
You make up the best parts
of my magical
fantastical fridge.
-H.C.

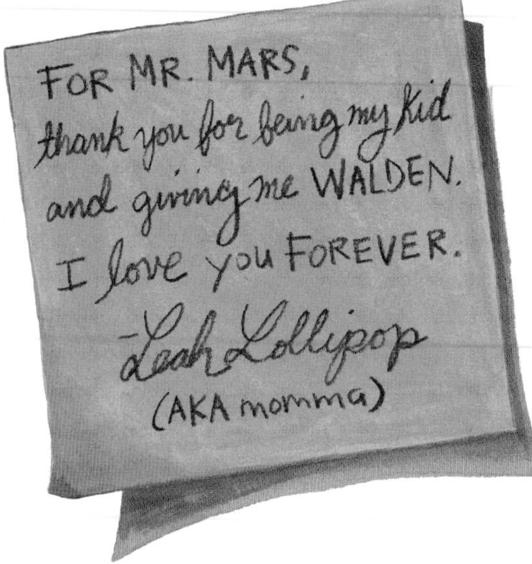

DIAL BOOKS FOR YOUNG READERS
Published by the Penguin Group
Penguin Group (USA) LLC
375 Hudson Street
New York, New York 10014

USA / Canada / UK / Ireland / Australia / New Zealand / India / South Africa / China
penguin.com
A Penguin Random House Company

Library of Congress Cataloging-in-Publication Data
Coben, Harlan, date.
The magical fantastical fridge / story by Harlan Coben ; pictures by Leah Tinari.
pages cm
Summary: When setting the table seems too boring, Walden takes off on an adventurous journey through all the pictures on his family's refrigerator.
ISBN 978-0-525-42803-9 (hardcover)
[1. Refrigerators—Fiction. 2. Adventure and adventurers—Fiction.] I. Tinari, Leah, illustrator. II. Title.
PZ7.C635Mag 2016
[E]—dc23 2015010837

Manufactured in China on acid-free paper
1 3 5 7 9 10 8 6 4 2

Designed by Lily Malcom
All text hand lettered by Leah Tinari

The art was created using pencil, pen, crayon, and gouache on Arches paper. It was also made with lots of love and the occasional hand cramp!

The Magical Fantastical Fridge

Story by Harlan Coben

Pictures by Leah Tinari

Dial Books for Young Readers

WALDEN
Time to
Set the table
for family dinner.
Grandma and PopPop
are on their way!

Aw MAN, so MANY plates!
ALL the aunts AND uncles
AND cousins...
Why do we *have* to do this
EVERY WEEKEND?

WALDEN, NOW Please!
I'M WALDEN THE BANDIT, and I don't set BORING tables in BORING houses. I NEED ADVENTURE! I want to be ANYWHERE but here. I wish I could just . . .
WALDEN
76
SMALL BUT MIGHTY

WHOA!
HEY, LET GO OF ME
WALDEN

Jersey Girl
WALDE
WHAT'S HAPPENING TO ME?
WHERE AM I ? Mom? DAD?
WAIT... I'm in my OWN drawing?

HEY, CRAYON MONSTER, put AWAY that sword! I drew you, REMEMBER?

STAND BACK, CRAYON MONSTER!
If you come any closer, I'll use my trusty... slice of PIZZA?
I'm going to fight a MONSTER with PIZZA?!
SMALL BUT MIGHTY

Uh-oh.
I'd better find a way OUT of HERE...
WAIT! THAT PLANE!

Hey, it's that **OLD** picture of Grandma and **PopPop** from before I was even born! Maybe if I time it right and let **GO** at the right second . . .

MAKE ART
NOT
WAR

I DID IT! Grandma, Pop Pop! I'm So happy to see you. You're NOT going to believe... HEY, what's with ALL the monkeys wearing SWEATERS? It's NOT that COLD!

Get these MONKEYS OFF of Me! I'll see you guys LATER! Like, LOTS and LOTS of years LATER!

CONEY
3460 1230
5
The AQUARIUM
is where I want
to BE.
CANNONBALL

Did I jump in here on "porpoise"?
I can"se
everythi
Oh "buoy," any-"fin" is possible today.
I can't hold my breath much longer. If you know a way out of here, let "minnow".
SPLASH

Hi, fish,
"water" you
thinking abo
Excuse me,
MR. PIRATE,
do you mind if I
BORROW your sword?
I need
air fast!

POP!
SMALL

Hey, it's my library card!
I'm making the letter N.
I wonder where this is
going to take me.

SMALL BUT MIGHTY!

The LIBRARY, OF COURSE! I go here with Grandma EVERY Thursday. LET me climb up here and get a BETTER look... OH YUM, FRIED CHICKEN!
Cooking
RANDALL
Medieval
Cooking
RANDALL
Medieval
Cooking

WAIT, WHAT THE....
I'M A CHICKEN
LEG!

OH MAN! What if SOMEONE gets hungry and EATS ME? I'd better hide. BUT WHERE?
HOLD ON, I KNOW...
SPARE
to
Strike
party!
for
Bowling
Saturday
union

NOBODY can See me NOW!
BIRTHDAY
SPARE TIME to Strike up a party!
for Penny's Bowling Bash
Saturday December 27th
3:00 - 5:00 pm
union square lanes
NYC

WHOA,
WHAT'S THAT RUMBLING SOUND?
It feels LIKE AN "EARTHQUAKE."
DON'T use the ICE MACHINE, MOM!!
CRASH
Ferdinando's
A

OH NO,
I THINK I'M
A PIN IN A
STRIKE!

"WATT'S" going on? THIS IS SHOCKING!
BUT "CURRENT"-LY I Love THIS!
HUGE ELECTRIC
411 S. CLINTON ST. SYRACUSE NY
PHONE: 2-1285
MONTHLY REPORT
SCOTT AVE NEW YORK
CALCULATED BASED ON EACH MONTH AT
MAY
JUNE
JULY
A B C D E

The POWER is surging through me. YIKES, the static ELECTRICITY is pulling me toward my sister, Celeste.
It's like a JUNGLE of HAIR in HERE. SMELLS nice, though. DON'T tell her I SAID THAT!
PARIS
ANCE

WOOF
WOOF
WHAT'S THAT NOISE? The game is ON! AH, I can HEAR IT. Grandma, PopPop, Cousin Eve, Céleste, UNCLE LARRY! Hello, can ANYONE HEAR ME?
JETS, JETS, JETS

The REFRIGERATOR is FUN, but I REALLY miss my FAMILY.
GO, GIANTS!
MAKE THE PASS!
JETS
12

Marlow & Sons
EST 2004
I WANT to go back home!
BUT HOW?
PARIS
FRANCE

If I could *just* get the SCISSORS from the *coupon*...

ON MY WAY HOME... I'M ALMOST FREE.

lanes

OKAY, just like in GYM CLASS.
TUCK, then ROLL, and...
RASH
Hello, KITCHEN FLOOR. Beautiful, WONDERFUL KITCHEN FLOOR! I love you, KITCHEN FLOOR.

WALDEN! Where have you BEEN?

It WAS *INCREDIBLE*, DAD! I was FIGHTING the CRAYON MONSTER with a PIZZA and *THEN* I was *swinging* from an AIRPLANE and then I was with *Grandma* and PopPop and the SWEATER monkeys . . .

WHOA, what an IMAGINATION! YOU'D BETTER *WASH UP*, *SON*. It's time for dinner.

FIRST I HAVE to set the table, or *Mom is* going to **FREAK**.

WHERE I WANT TO GO
AFRICA
JAPAN
BRAZIL
ITALY
LOVE
WALDEN
XO
JULIAN HENRY
THEO RAMONA
JACOB BELLA
REY ESTELLE
ODIN
QUINN AIDAN

Shipwrecks and Pioneer Cemeteries
PRINCE EDWARD ISLAND
RADIO CITY BIG STAR
olly
PICASSO
FATTA

I'M BACK in the best PLACE
in the WHOLE WORLD.
At home with my family.

CWS
Bronx
NEW YORK
FLYING
GLIDERS
1+4=5
Jersey Girl
REBELS
33
WaLDen
16
Ferdinando's
Focacceria Rosticceria
Cucina Siciliana
A